Praise for the Work of Jimmy Santiago Baca

"Stands as proof there is always hope in even the most desperate lives."
—*Fort Worth Morning Star-Telegram* on *A Place to Stand*

"This slim, salient volume will open readers' eyes wide to the true human stories behind blaring headlines about immigration policies and debates."
—*Booklist*, starred review, on *When I Walk through That Door, I Am: An Immigrant Mother's Quest*

"Incredibly emotive and beautifully written. A must read."
—*Bustle* on *When I Walk through That Door, I Am*

"Jimmy Baca's new book brilliantly reimagines the epic poem—and reshapes the epic hero as a young immigrant woman struggling to escape violence and find the child that has been torn away from her. A work that speaks strikingly and passionately of our times."
—Richard Blanco on *When I Walk Through That Door, I Am*

"[Baca's] voice, brutal and tender, is unique in America."
—Ilan Stavans, *The Nation*

"What makes [Baca's poetry] a success is its honesty, a brutal honesty, as well as his original imagery and the passion of his writing."
—Gary Soto, *The San Francisco Chronicle*

"To read Jimmy Santiago Baca's poetry is to tramp across the uneven terrain of human experience, sometimes lulled by the everydayness of work or relationships, and then dazzled by a flood of emotion or vibrant observation."
—*Western American Literature*

T0046389

"[With *A Glass of Water*] Baca manages to put a face on desperation. He decries the exploitation of migrant farm workers in the United States . . . [and] derogates not only an exploitive American economic system, but also Mexican drug lords driving the poor off their land, who become homeless or victims of violence. . . . [But] a field worker's life isn't all toil and gloom as reflected in the lives of the characters. There's also passion, joy, love of family, adventure, love, longing, and accomplishment. The imagery is striking, the prose lyrical."

—*The Albuquerque Journal*

"[A] blistering novel . . . The sheer passion that drives Baca's [work] is undeniable."

—*Publishers Weekly* on *A Glass of Water*

Baca "writes with unconcealed passion" and "manifests both an intense lyricism and that transformative vision which perceives the mythical and archetypal significance of life events."

—Denise Levertov

no enemies
poems

Jimmy Santiago Baca

Arte Público Press
Houston, Texas

No Enemies is made possible through a grant from the National Endowment for the Arts. We are thankful for its support.

Recovering the past, creating the future

Arte Público Press
University of Houston
4902 Gulf Fwy, Bldg 19, Rm 100
Houston, Texas 77204-2004

Cover design by Mora Des¡gn
Cover photo by Lonnie J. Anderson

Names: Baca, Jimmy Santiago, 1952- author.
Title: No enemies : poems / Jimmy Santiago Baca.
Description: Houston, Texas : Arte Publico Press, [2021] | Summary: "Acclaimed poet Jimmy Santiago Baca knows something is wrong with contemporary society. He's afraid "that the whole network / that connects us / and society together / is going to collapse / that our lives / will be dependent on tiny / little blue wires / that can't shake my hand / or share my joy, / that won't challenge the police / to stop beating a brown man / or can't do even something as small / and gentle as smile." In this collection of new poems, Baca expresses his sense of responsibility to use his gift for the greater good. "If not me, then who / speaks to money, power, privilege / if not / an ordinary man / then who?" He chastises those who use their connections to benefit themselves at the expense of the impoverished, imprisoned and undocumented. Frequently, he takes aim at poets and politicians who put their lucrative positions ahead of their constituents: "Governor, if you choose a career / where you have to ignore the truth / and pillage the unfortunate, at least / outlaw automatic weapons." While many of these poems are stinging rebukes against the wealthy and powerful and their disregard for children living in poverty and the environment, others are beautiful odes to his indigenous roots. There are buffalo with their gentle hearts, sacred places where he prays to his ancestors and the plants growing on steep mountainsides that give "me courage to keep clinging to hope and to learn / life's most important lesson / practice how to lean in life so as not to fall." Baca writes urgently about the most important themes of our generation, including education, justice, the environment and even the coronavirus. Ironically, he notes, "the enemy didn't come at us crossing borders, / swinging machetes and machine guns." No, nature herself has come to clean house, to give "Mother Earth a reprieve from our greed." —Provided by publisher.
Identifiers: LCCN 2021028086 (print) | LCCN 2021028087 (ebook) |
    ISBN 9781558859272 (trade paperback ; alk. paper) |
    ISBN 9781518506710 (epub) | ISBN 9781518506727 (kindle edition) |
    ISBN 9781518506734 (pdf)
Subjects: LCGFT: Poetry.
Classification: LCC PS3552.A254 N6 2021 (print) | LCC PS3552.A254 (ebook) |
    DDC 811/.54—dc23
LC record available at https://lccn.loc.gov/2021028086
LC ebook record available at https://lccn.loc.gov/2021028087

21 22 23   4 3 2 1

CONTENTS

POETRY

EDUCATION

A SACK OF POTATOES, A BOWL OF APPLES

ALLOW THE ANGELS IN

WILDLIFE

Acknowledgements

As always, none of these poems would be possible if not for the love from so many people I believe in who work in our communities and barrios for justice, education, health care. Seeing you do the real work, teachers, poets/writers, painters, *santeros*, dancers, so many everyday people, inspires me. And of course, my *familia*, my beautiful kids Tones, Gabe, Esai and Lucía, without you, nothing is possible. Last but most pivotal, my beautiful wife Stacy.

NO ENEMIES

By Charles Mackay
(English Chartist poet, 1814-1889)

YOU have no enemies, you say?
Alas! my friend, the boast is poor.
He who has mingled in the fray
of duty that the brave endure,
must have made foes. If you have none,
small is the work that you have done.
You've hit no traitor on the hip.
You've dashed no cup from perjured lip.
You've never turned the wrong to right.
You've been a coward in the fight.

POLITICS

History books praise them, colonial poets
claim them bravest, evangelicals
label them saviors and redeemers
but I beg to differ with Whitman and President Polk
and others who mythologize wagon-train white settlers
as heroes. Or put another way:
How about you have them
rape your mother and daughter
sell your son into slavery
steal your land
burn your house
lynch your father, then
call them heroes.
Write about them as romantic cowboys in western novels
lionize them in films *How the West Was Won.*
Trapper, military genius, explorers
Missouri & Ohio pioneers, western heroes
white historical figures your kids
can emulate and look up to:
the Bents, Fremonts, Carsons, Kearnys . . .

How about that?

Days of broken glass and bloody needles
junkies throw in parks and yards
days when poets are picketed at readings
and political discourse is settled
with pipe bombs and shootings
days of burning crosses by white nationalists
urged and commended by a president
encouraging violence and rancor and division,
these are the days
when no child can find a leader to admire.

Days of broken glass and bloody needles
dogs shred their paws and barefoot children
contract AIDS
days of broken glass and bloody needles
when speech and words have become useless
and mayors use educational resources to support
guns and clubs and police forces
and militarized goon squads,
these are days
when the singers have had their tongues cut out
and clergy sodomize trusting children.

Days of broken glass and bloody needles
when shahs, monarchs, dictators
bomb cities of women and children
when right-wing extremists claim
all who are not White
should be imprisoned, shot, turned away
starved and maligned.

These are days of broken glass and bloody needles
when even our finest writers and celebrity TV hosts
prey on women, days of broken glass and bloody needles
broken glass and bloody needles
broken glass and bloody needles. . . .

There was a time when things
were held together
with mud, rock, wire, hand
instead of beeps, LEDs, passwords.

There's a fear in me
a warning that the breakdown
is coming
that the whole network
that connects us
and society together
is going to collapse
that our lives
will be dependent on tiny
little blue wires
that can't shake my hand
or share my joy
that won't challenge a policeman
to stop beating a brown man
or can't do even something as small
and gentle as smile.

Our whole lives
depend on blue little wires,
these little computer boards
and silver wires
that direct military wars and drones
dismiss baby turtles crossing the road
in Myanmar, thousands murdered
by military convoys on their way
to quell protests for justice.

There is something very wrong
going on, I feel it.

൙ ൙

All of this happens in the space of two hours:
A Movie on Netflix, titled *New Bulletin*, streams a banner that
scrolls left to right on screen:

*545 white children forcibly separated from parents in Idaho
cannot be found.*

*New report shows hundreds of cases in which the deported white
parents of children who were taken from their families cannot be
located.*

Meanwhile, same time, in black and white reality, in downtown
Albuquerque, Mario Cortez, 19, is unable to hold his head up for
a mug shot, the police send him to the hospital, where doctors
diagnose a crushed vertebra and a body temperature of 82.4
degrees. He spends the next several weeks on a ventilator and dies
on July 15. From the visitor's waiting area, at Central and Univer-
sity, all the way to the foothills, you hear his little brother and sis-
ter and mother wailing. No protests, no investigation, no news
story, just one more fresh grave of the hundreds down at the ceme-
tery, almost all Mexicans and Chicanos.

Meanwhile, same time, 17-year-old Stavian Rodríguez is mur-
dered, shot twelve times by five police officers.

Meanwhile, same time, in a University of New Mexico campus
apartment a poet composes this poem.

❦ ❧

Dread, dressed in police uniforms, Border Patrol and ICE uniforms,
stalks our doorstep. We are afraid to open our doors. We don't come out,
we hide in our homes from the world beyond our home that hunts us.
We pray the violence goes away. Confused by messages
from politicians, we pray the Lord speaks to us with a clear voice.
Tell us what to do, Lord.
What do we do, Lord, when they're killing our kids,
the police, Border Patrol, ICE, vigilante white death-squads,
Mexican drug lords and dealers, killing our families.
Tell us. Lord, guide us, comfort us. Lord, which way
do we go from here?

Dread stalks our doorstep, we are afraid to open our doors.

Meanwhile, in countless homes the Netflix movie ends,
viewers on couches sit stunned by the rash kidnappings
of white people
depicted on screen.

There was a time
you cared about the future.
What you did today was gauged
by its impact on the future for our kids,
neighbors, communities . . .
tomorrow meant something.

But with your riches and fame
you've lost your accountability.

Getting your nails and hair done for your poodle,
spending a small ransom
to buy a Gulf Stream Jet to avoid rush-hour traffic,
gold-plating your bathroom handles,
on your ninth nose lift, importing ivory rhino tusk-
diamond necklaces and bracelets . . . Well,
I suppose they're good sound barriers
to keep those cries of the falsely imprisoned
from you hearing them.

                                        I guess.

You keep inviting me to your posh getaway
down at your Mexican hideout. It's one big
spa, you brag, servant quarters, gardeners, cooks, maids. . . .
You expound your new philosophy
is to grab and smash, get as much as you can
regardless of environmental consequence
or harm to others. If you don't someone else will, you boast,
the whole society is a riot zone, those Black Lives Matter
and Chicanos burning buildings, carrying big screens,
video games and blocks of toilet paper
down the street, they understand—get
what you can for yourself, take what you can carry,
that's what the rich teach the poor—and it helps,

while you're getting, to convey a good Samaritan countenance
in press conferences, photo-ops, project that you care,
implore others to donate with those big brown eyes of yours,
makes a good story, helps to spread your unbelievable goodness
in literary magazines and journals, social news organizations,
all those thank-you Hallmark cards you send out thanking
your wealthy patrons, while that smile of yours keeps working
                              overtime. Get it while you can.

Governor, if you choose a career
where you have to ignore the truth
and pillage the unfortunate, at least
                outlaw automatic weapons.

A career where the food you eat
clothes you wear
schools your children attend
jewels your wife sparkles in
saunas you relax in
homes you sleep safely in
are all bought and paid for by people
working their asses off out here
struggling to pay utilities in the real world
and put food on the table, at least
                outlaw automatic weapons.

A career where greed and deception
are necessary tools of the trade
as mother's milk to a babe.

Alabama, Missouri, Mississippi, Georgia, Idaho, Dakotas . . .
              what made these insurrectionists
so damn mean
unhappy and brutish, why, when they
have been given three hundred years
of privileged convenience, when the government
gave them slaves, free land, the right
to make their own rules and laws
made sure they got the best loans
the exclusive good-old-boy deals, why are they so unhappy

so cruel, willing to walk into
a Baptist church or elementary school
and murder the innocent, even riot in our capitol?
              Why
does some sinister cancer eat away at their souls
some leprous gangrene rots out their hearts
what is it, that makes them collect
AR-15s, stockpile weapons, hate so much, drooling
to kill and maim so many innocent people?

Windchimes:
bankers blowing the way wind blows
at the end of a money-string

NRA gun medals
dangling from the porch rafter of the Florida pipe bomb madman

hanging in Jair Bolsonaro's eunuched crotch
from the canopy frame of the orange-haired clown's golf cart

Crown Prince Mohammed bin Salman
of Saudi Arabia's beard

from the mics of loud angry white guys on am radio screaming
                                        blowing the way wind blows.

Just back from a trip
with family
to San Francisco.
A week later
the morning starts
with a visit to the doctor—
colon-aahhhhss-copy
the word sounds like a crusty-tempered
scorpion.
Innards clean
as newly installed copper piping.
Then my son wrecks the car
I just bought him.
The dealership
says it'll cost 1,600 to fix—
I have to pay 500
my insurance covers the rest.
On the way back from checking out
the car,
I stop, fill up my truck near Kirtland air force base.
At home I realize I don't have my wallet,
I drive back to the station,
ask the attendant
has anyone turned in my wallet?
I check around the bays,
find it on top of the gas pump I used,
money gone but cards still in,
surprised a soldier stole my money—
so much for the character of our troops.

Later, bummed I lost our Christmas money
but still have my license, do what I do when I'm pissed:
watch TV, the Peloton lady on the commercial
with those big brown eyes

convinces me she has the answers
to my holiday worries, if I buy a bike and ride it,
money will pour from the skies, if I buy a Peloton
it'll end my misery, if I buy one I can have
a personal relationship with it and be happy,
if I buy one I can improve every aspect of my life.
                    I buy.

Afterwards, when she sees how much it costs,
my wife goes into a depression.
I promise to buy a winning lottery ticket
because I was going to get dental work done
but it costs ten grand for the procedure,
my co-pay is 9 thousand 900 dollars
with Delta—a serious rip-off—
but we Americans are used to getting shafted. . . .
Just think of the pale-skinned blond-haired
maggot, the biggest rip-off in the history of America. . . .
We'll be paying for his greed and lies for generations.

                         What's the co-pay on that,
                         totally destroying
                         your child's future?

If not me, then who
speaks
to money, power, privilege?
If not
an ordinary man,
then who?

I bus inner-city children
to the forest to see migrating birds,
the bear's prints
in the snow, track the turkeys,
take them snowshoeing,
let them study the eagle's
feathers on a pine branch nest. . . .
If not me, who?

Early October, time to turn on
the heater, the sprinklers off,
dogs roughhouse enjoying the chill.
If not me, who
will speak for those
who have never seen
these simple sights?

A white rattler separates families,
jams children in cages along the border,
displays fanged-flags from southern porches,
claiming themselves patriots—
after all the crimes of their ancestors—the lynching,
murdering, pillaging, rapes of my indigenous/Mexican people,
their wealth built on robbing us,
breaking laws and Mexican treaties,
disregarding human decency. . . .
Who, if not me, will unveil the lie,

strip away the smile on presidential faces,
extract the poisonous fangs dripping with our blood?

Dawn fills with balloons
bobbing across the Albuquerque sky
in early October . . . Rained heavy last night, enough
thunder to get the dogs barking
and running under beds.

While balloon goers and balloon flyers
enjoy their leisure, at the New Mexico border
evil prowls and devours brown people
taken by THE WALL:

seedless grapes shrivel, raspberries blacken,
apples wrinkle, pears stunted,
chickens decay, cow bones litter the desert,
avocado hulls harden,
soup bowls fill with sand,
cheese string wrappers and almond milk cartons
clot with insects—death by corporation.

Beyond the death-scape,
border wall construction workers
deploy monster equipment
to destroy archaeological sites,
massive generators suck every drop
of ground water to make more cement
to build the wall higher,
heavy machinery growls smoke and roars,
cannibalizing cacti, trees, shrubs,
                                        killing
                                        killing
                                        killing.

If not me, who will speak for you?

ೲ ೲ

Re-entry has become so dangerous
for ex-cons
the Department of Transportation
has erected ex-con re-entry road signs
next to wildlife crossing signs.

Voting season,
ex-cons suffering trauma
of having been caged, avoid booths,
use gas station bathroom walls
to vote.

∽❧ ❧∼

Among you fellow citizens there are those
who turn on me
with anti-immigration hatred,
scapegoat me,
perpetrate violence against me,
rally mob, spout propaganda, move against me,
attack me as an enemy, round me up out of life,
out of job, out of school, strip my citizenship,
forbid my interracial marriage,
classify me an outsider, non-human,
no employment rights, no legal rights,
used me as a testing ground for eugenics,
anti-immigrant policies, experiment on me,
lock me in your outdoor cage,
get me out, drive me out, no place to go,
the wrath of racists declare war on me,
frenzied mobs drool hatred toward me,
domestic terrorists steal my property, my items of value
looted by crazed patriots who unleash hell on me,
burn my house, kill my family, beat me to death,
destroy me, wage war on me,
take me to camp, keep me in custody,
                    call it their America.

⁓◌ ◌⁓

Wikipedia: "Since the 16th century, Lady Justice has often been depicted wearing a blindfold. The blindfold represents impartiality, the ideal that justice should be applied without regard to wealth, power, or other status."
Waiting
I remember it was a game—blindfolded,
an adult handed me a broomstick,
turned me round until wobbly-dizzy,
swung a few times,
then whack I smacked *la piñata*,
candy and kids scattered everywhere
                                    hysterically
blinded by the bounty.

Also, blindfolded,
we played touch and you're it:
arms extended, grope air,
teased by lunging giggles, back out of reach
lunge, miss, miss, finally I touch another kid
and he's it.

These games, I understood.

This Lady Justice, blindfolded, I don't.
Was she kidnapped?
I'll pay her ransom
to get her back, to get her to drop the blindfold
so she can see again, and we don't
have to go far— no ISIS, Al Qaeda, Boko Haram.
In Albuquerque, Central Avenue, police murdered
Luis Montoya last night, two other cops raped
María Quintana on the Westside mesa.

Lady Justice, you have a comfortable way
to inhabit time, in your righteousness,
understanding life only in terms of your darkness,
do you not feel an irremediable loss and sadness
over what the rich white racists have done to you?

Better to have junkies steal those scales,
melt them in the furnace of a closed steel mill
into gold rings and bracelets
than for you to go on pretending you care.
We wait while the wealthy
ruin this country, while police rulers
rent out jail cells to the poor and corporate
oligarchs spread your legs
in judges' chambers and repeatedly rape you.

You've been silent too long,
time for the blindfolds to come off,
look around at your people,
La Raza, who wander
in your shadow homeless refugees
waiting for you to untie the knot and throw that rag
away, swing the razor-edged scales on that chain
as if they were samurai weapons and cut and slice at injustice.

I can help.
I can teach you to take my hand.
You don't have to be afraid,
you don't have to be in denial, we can both,
with three hundred million others
teach you to see again, to give you
a life again that explains why you are here
holding those golden scales as you do.

Right now,
those scales are weighed down, rusting away,
holding Wall Street yachts in one, poor in the other. . . .

Shake 'em! Shake 'em! Free 'em up!

So you can accurately weigh the weight
of my humanity against injustice, get the precise
reading of my suffering against their riches,
correctly measure my life's worth
and dreams for a better life
against corrupt judges and corporate oppressors.

Turn your scales to catch the sun's reflection,
illuminate my dreams again with hope,
let your light rays shoot into the alleys,
jail cells, under bridges, hospitals, old age homes,
food lines, on teenage sex-slaves trafficked
and runaways fucking privileged men for a hamburger and fries.

Wake the fuck up, Lady!

cᘓ ᘐᕽ

You've been posing way too long,
pretending to represent
people like me living week to week.
Take a bath, brush your hair, look presentable,
there's a lot of us waiting for you,
we can help you, take that blindfold off
                           and see us.

We've been at it a long time.
You can join us in the lines
marching, protesting, fasting, striking,
you don't have to be afraid. Sure, you might
get bruised, gassed, pepper-sprayed,
end up getting arrested, beat up, maybe even killed,
but we can free you, we can make you feel alive,
vibrant, and we'll show you how beautiful you really are,
how much you're loved when you're with us.
                                  We're ready.

∽◉ ◎∾

9 to 5 workweek for a paycheck.
I hold my palms up to the sun
each morning,
pray it fills them with a new direction.

Each day I create a statue
of loneliness—the doubt, the sorrow, the hope,
ingrained and chiseled into the surface.

I want my life
a book of pages that flutter away in the wind,
that sail across fields.
Who can teach me this?
Who can guide me to such a teacher?

Exhausted, spent, depleted, my life wasted
at this 9 to 5 job, living bill to bill,
an unholy enterprise that drives me to be
too afraid to offend anyone,
willing to reinforce my boss' view,
write what pleases them,
send holiday gift cards and thank yous
to all who pay me to ensure
I keep them smiling
with my servile gratitude,
make sure to please them
at every opportunity,
accept the dinner invites,
have coffee with them,
meet important people and stand
next to them as someone of color,
someone from the poor side,
someone who suffered and persevered,
someone they point

to brag they have a Mexican friend,
live up to that token symbol
in the pics and handshakes and award ceremonies,
be that for them who need me
to pose for them, who need me to obey,
who need me to say yes, as they pick me up
and move me to the next square on the chess board
that enables them to keep playing me for their recreation.

White privilege has convinced me,
after the Kavanaugh hearings,
I'm ready to start voting for animals:
my Mastiff and Corso
for judge and mayor—no joke.
What my eyes see and my ears hear
my mind and heart can't believe.

Today I am going to the cemetery
to bury my copy of the constitution,
the 14th amendment,
mashed and dirtied and wrinkled
after having been used for a napkin
to wipe the chins and hands and mouths
of white privileged men
who gorge at the trough of money and power.

We all know hell
has fire, but what else?
Windows? Kitchen? Bed with a room?
Sign me up, it's better than I have
here in this neighborhood
where kids can't even get to school
without getting shot by cops.

cৎ৩ ৩৶

for Oliver Bruno & his Congregation

America
your betrayal
forced my eyes wide open
I don't know
if I can ever close them again.

I sleep with eyes wide open.

·

My voice flowers up
from the buried, the hidden, the secret . . .
words
embedded in the nightmares
of the sleepless,
where I blossom.

·

I can't turn back time.
Were a clock somewhere
to halt time, I would
stop the migrant caravan
traveling two thousand miles
only to be caged in dog kennels
to watch their children die.
                              I would go back,
tell them stop, you don't know what awaits you
but I know—
dreams are stronger than any warning,
stronger than the threat of death.
                              When one dreams

one is alive, and when one doesn't
one is dead.

•

Know me by my dreaming
not my fingerprints,
not my face in a church basement
as a refugee.

∽⊙ ⊙∾

Even as your ICE officials bang
against this poem like glass and break doors
to get in,
I sing, above the women and children's screams

I sing

Even as they drag us out the back door
handcuff children too

I sing.

Lord, my savior Jesus, be with me on this journey,
when they arrest me they arrest you.
America has closed its doors on me.
You have opened yours, oh Lord,
even though they withhold my citizenship documents
You offer yours, oh Lord, and welcome me,
embrace me, soothe my fears,
and even as they criminalize me, You, oh Lord,
celebrate my innocence and I laugh in your light.
I am free, oh Lord, in Your love
and I sing in Spanish, We Shall Not Be Moved
and Amazing Grace, Amazing Grace . . .

We don't need a July 4th celebration.
Seems like anyone who can
shoot, inject, slice, smoke, bludgeon,
snort and bomb is a patriot.

It's an American pastime
all over the city, every night,
neighborhoods
snarl, hiss,
color trails stream
spread across the night—
cops light fireworks,
blue, red, yellow, green flash
sparklers burning bright
as road crews and police cadets
in yellow parkas and badged caps
clean up crashes—glass, molded plastic swept,
tow trucks haul away gnarled iron,
drunks, addicts, tweaker corpses
scraped and swept off the asphalt,
warning sparklers burn bright.
Every night is a holiday of fools
in our city.

Black brothers and sisters
I'll give you some of my brown
if you give me some of your black.
Plant this biracial seed of our new beginning
into everything we do, into school, sports,
health care, justice,
together, united, some of your Asian honey complexion
and some of my brown mixed up
to grow a new biracial literature, poetry, music, art.
Lock arms and march baby march.
Give me some Caribbean gold and I'll give you some brown.
My voice your voice, my hand your hand
refuse to separate what God has joined,
some of my brown and some of your black,
my brown for Asian honey color, my brown
for your Caribbean almond, no more hurting each other,
no more killing, no more fighting, no more.
Let's give birth to each other, let's unite,
larger, stronger, fresher than when we were alone
and make some of the most amazing colors,
amazing words, braiding songs
into biracial blessings, some of the most amazing blessings.

cە ەد

for Seema

In praise of poets
unafraid of writing political poems
your poems an outcry against the madness
that has seized upon the American heart
made it a violent and uncontrollable gallop
toward extreme injustice, mayhem, unassailable
reign of chaos that seeks to kill what is powerless and innocent,
take and take and take what will feed its continuing
craving for power and wealth. . . . If you must, dear reader,
stop a passerby, hail pedestrians to pause on the sidewalk,
hand them a book of verse for free and tell them
with a smile, read it, it will enrich and elevate your life,
give purpose to your waking on this day
a necessary ritual that takes us back
to our conscious humanity and humble empowerment. . . . Bravo!

POETRY

cઠ ઠ

To be a poet you must have gratefulness
at the center of your mission to write.

The poem is a witness,
transcends trend,
channels change,
the skin
that wraps a human heart
grounding what beats within.

A certain gravity
exists beneath words
in the space between them,
pulls our life in
where sacred budding starts,
and transformation takes.

A mirage works for a wanderer in the desert,
beckons you onward when you're most lost.
Poetry works for me like that.

ఴ ఱ

If a book walked up and slapped
one of those young white publishers
upside the head
they still wouldn't know what good
poetry is. They publish safe poetry,
cake-recipe poems, girl-scout cookie-dough poems,
kitchen-apron poetry, yessum-master poetry,
not the steer butchering bloody poetry
cooked outside over campfires
shared and fed to all who have worked
a day in the heat and cold
and toiled for the love of it
to help out a friend.

Somehow I've lost touch with why
I write. Two days in a row now
I've gone on national TV and social media
reading friends' poems, my cronyism
somewhat embarrassing—it's a little
weird, incestuous, nepotistic—my critics point out
the interbreeding procreates weak poetics,
turns our writing and reading each other's poems on
national Latina radio programs, even in some cities
erecting statues to each other, quad plates on university statues
commemorate my campus visit,
hotel rooms are given my name,
parks, libraries, schools too . . . I'm relaxing,
dressed up for my Saturday afternoon Diego Rivera
and Frida Kahlo tea-hour
waiting for my friends to arrive.

When I was born, if my throat had been cut instead of my navel cord,
I would not have fallen into so many troubles, or undergone so many hardships.
> —Sheikh Farid Ji, Sri Guru Granth Sahib

Lament of a poet out of favor:
No more will I mock myself
with these shmoozefests—
that's the word that
comes to mind
when I see myself in online pics
cradling my trophies and checks,
no longer reviewing a book's worth
by its contents
but by friendships and gender and ethnicity
politically correct or social networks,
not the poem's worth.

I've been seduced by the media and the publishers
awash in money to promote me,
make me seem popular, that my books are great,
when in fact, on more occasions than I care to think about
my books have failed at every turn to engage my mind
with awe, surprise, love, meaning.
Same ole same ole trite rehashing of topics
that show no courage or risk or innovativeness
than a block of ice.
                              Shmoozefests.

The second they don't need me,
don't turn to me for their ethnic quota validation.
I am remitted to the has-been bin,
no longer useful to them,
         no longer belong to the clique,
         no longer acceptable—

ignored, ostracized, exiled
from their lunches,
deciding what poets should be laureates,
picking ones who comfort
the rich, praise the powerful,
following behind their white masters.

Mainstream America had me believe
if they string a few promises together
it makes up for the injustice
for the school-to-prison pipeline system,
for the trashing of our environment,
for illiteracy among people of color,
mainstream murmuring clichés in photo-ops
while Israelis kill Palestinian children,
and poet laureates in headbands
keep dismissing the truth that earth
is old and wrinkled and sunken-faced in her misery,
has become a sinkhole withdrawn from the light. . . .

Here it is, Mainstream, my oath:
I will not spend my time
kissing ass,
nor waste a whole life bending down
to the master with the checkbook.
If I get to the edge where I'm starving,
                              I'll eat these pages.

for Alfred Cisneros

My friend Alfred, disappeared, left his nice house,
friends, obligations, vanished almost four years ago,
no sign, no evidence, no clue, nothing but this note left on his desk:

Confessions of a Media Darling:
I used to be a—Bang for the Buck—writer,
it was too much, always in the news, a prize chaser,
a company poet, a devout philanthropy worshiper,
literary mobster, scholarly gang-banger
snuffing out the competition with blacklist, false rumors,
gossip weapons.
It was too much,
ah yes, a Media Darling
with all my headlines
and still,
I was unknown in the community,
                    mothers did not know me,
the poor, the workers, the hopeless, the dreamers
my name and books were foreign to them,
only the rich knew me, the ones who gave out awards
and hosted national radio programs.
                    The rich and powerful
kept telling me how good my novels were
but no one here has heard of me.

Did I write of prison reform,
criminal justice reform,
did my work grieve the death of millions
of trees in tropical forests, millions
of birds gone extinct, millions

of children suffering poverty in the barrio?
No, I praised the wealthy, I knew Oprah, was given
a presidential medal, I wrote,
I chanted yoga mantras, I socialized with the upper crust,
recited culturally exotic Mexican ditties
to entertain elite officials,
wrote for white approval, an FDA government-
stamped writer with an expiration date.

And at night before slept I knew
what I described had no feeling, no blood
filled my words, just a clear, bitter liquid of reason,
not connected to heart or soul, well-aware
reviewers pay you homage for ideas not empathy,
the rich promote you, foundations hype your importance,
because of what you're not writing.
Mothers, sisters, brothers, grandparents
in the barrio did not know me.

As a boy, my mother told me
real poets are scarce, they scare
the wealthy and powerful.
My mother said real poets roar their poems
from an angry youthful heart, real poets my mother said
reveal, ignite, provoke. . . .

And we would sit on the couch for hours
while she read me poems from Hernández, about an onion
and we cried, the mother and babe that only had
an onion to eat, for the husband and father imprisoned for his
    beliefs.

As a man one morning, off to meet a friend running for public office,
I paused before the hallway mirror to check how I looked
in my new suit, my gold watch and ring, and saw myself—

the false smile, my cook in the kitchen, my gardeners,
my servant and maid about cleaning up,
and my cheeks paled, my eye disgraced
by the memory of my mother.
What check, my heart asked my soul,
will pay for your silence?
So goodbye, my dear friends,
I'm off to find my soul.

↍‘ ‘↍

The heart is a museum of natural history
parts of poems hang from hooks and wires
from the ceiling—
skeletal, screwed joints, glued razor teeth, clamped jaws.
The poet works these parts
keeps them fed, clothed, sheltered
                    until they come alive
                    and roar.

A hard long week
means every stone in my house
is a poem I lifted, placed, secured
to keep me warm from the cold,
sheltered from the wild.
Every log in my cabin I bought writing poetry.
Every shoe and dress and pair of pants and shirt
paid for with poetry. Never took the offers
to teach at universities, though, must be one Chicano
who can make it on his writing, one Chicano
who can stand outside the esteemed roundtable
of learned geniuses and proclaim himself a poet,
who needs to prove he can make it as a poet, earn
his food and upkeep, raise five kids,
a Chicano poet who works with his hands and heart,
who declines university posts, distinguished chairs,
not because he doesn't want them, but to prove
like white and black writers, that a Chicano can survive
and succeed and flourish as a poet on the power
of his poems, against all the university presidents who thought
    me too radical,
all the philanthropies and foundations who thought me dangerous
and honored other poets with money because of their submissive
    temperaments,
to prove a Chicano poet could keep his integrity, his courage,
write in the face of denials and censorship, write
in the face of poverty and being an outcast, write
despite being scorned and neglected
because I was thought to be too threatening to the powers,
too wild, too disobedient, too contrary
to their wanting to make the rules and control me
with regulations. To be accepted they said
I must bow before them, mostly all white, and I refused.

There had to be one Chicano who could make it,
                                    and I did,
                                    fifty years later.
                                    Thank you, poetry,
for giving me a good life.

My father said, always have good shoes and good teeth
no matter where you go in life, where you leave and arrive, do so
with good shoes and teeth,
and he forgot to say, which I add, and a poem.

∾ ∾

I'm tired of me,
of seeing myself on BIG READ library posters
morning news reporters on NPR
start off reading my poem
on another disappointed white man
entering a car-parts store
killing everyone.
I've become a hooray poet, an effigy
of who I really am.
The key has always been
to take the wildness in me,
and in that quiet taming
comes the poem.

My prayer:
let my body write the poem,
let it meet the page in sheer rawness,
in the way high surf hits rocks.
Let my compositions be exuberant,
let flesh and bones and muscle write the poem
so you know what I feel, so I bring you in
to see how I see the world.

❦ ❧

Writers work,
pay rent, health insurance,
buy clothes, eat,
pay utilities, must

work,
dig heels in, ankles, thighs, hips down
in the mud, push books, advertise them,
sail high and wide with bright colors,
visit schools and after, when
the pushing is done, move on,
they return to obscurity, to their books,
the bulwark against oblivion.
Let the intent of our goodness
be the weapon that disarms our enemies.

cø ⁊

Bullets in Bodies

In most countries,
poets proudly point out the bullets
embedded in their bodies—shot
for speaking what they believe or write—
bullets birthed by words
they could not hold back,
words they had to speak,
words they had to love,
words they sent out
to embrace the frightened children.

I've met six of them from other countries.
We'd be sitting around a table
and one of them sometimes pushes
one to the surface,
pushes it up out of the flesh,
years of much distracted thumbing, and it finally comes up,
and when it does, it becomes a gift for the wife,
who makes bracelets from the bullets,
necklaces, wears them grateful her man
is alive, or as a legacy passed down to children
to say, "This was your father's gift to you,"
as symbols to speak up, to be fearless,
to fight for freedom, to struggle for peace.

In America, few poets have bullets in their bodies.

In America, poets wear flashy designer clothes,
drive new cars, have no rap sheets for anti-government
non-violence protest. No, most are clean, sterile,
no civil disobedience records,
blemished antiseptic lives, new as gleaming silverware.
Most have never even jay-walked, most

are corporate-sponsored, company poets,
rarely raise their voices in anger,
instead
display their certificates, awards
to admiring officials,
but few carry bullets in their bodies
where they have been shot
for saying or writing what they believed.

After my reading, during Q&A,
this poet stood and asked
may I read a poem?
I said sure.

Words present me a prism
a unique perspective
to see things differently.
You're never saved.
You work, grow, struggle
deal with situations,
piss people off, dirty your hands,
have no answers—a witness to
to dash to dust
the hierarchy of fools.

Poets get mean
not rich,
not endear themselves to the benefactors,
not curtsey or bow or humiliate themselves. . . .

They make mistakes, have a murky past,
lust, hate, are lonely, full of life, verve, passion . . .

serve refugees, separated parents, the imprisoned,
lack health insurance,
rage like a hawk caught in a net

                                            against injustice.

~❧ ❧~

Another poet stood up and read:
There are those in search of gold
in search of themselves, in search of purpose,
who wish to grab the light,
hold it in their hands,
take it with them like a bar of gold
they don't know yet.
Love is transitory. Worship
what the hand can pass through,
feel, if for a moment,
the heat in your palm.

This bearded poet in San Francisco
in the audience stated,
I'm a great teacher but they always ask
for a résumé. For once in my life
I'd like to say stop with the résumé stuff!
Tell me, how do you update a résumé of a life
lived on the margins, outside society,
doing what society considers a waste of time
supporting five kids and a wife
on the paltry wages of a poet
who refuses to compromise
by signing his soul off on the dotted line
to a philanthropist with a check or a bureaucracy
with an official position or an organization
ready to pump steroids into an advertising campaign
to package you off as the greatest poet or writer
of your generation?

What kind of résumé would be in order?

He went on to say,
there's a trend toward poor-me books
flooding the market, poets/writers
affecting a whimsical feminine posture
among literary elites and foundation boards
on the one hand, but on stage,
before a real audience of students and readers,
try to be cool   ·
morph into a mixture of John Wayne and Rambo,
cursing, projecting themselves out to the public
as the new outlaw poets.

I've lived beyond rules and regulations,
no careerist or coronation—don't

need you or anyone to appoint me a poet,
wealthy fat-cats, philanthropists, publishers, foundations
crowning me a great poet—no literary knighthood here,
my verse
labeled as rebellious, outlaw defiance,
has forged its way out of the cardboard box
that doubled as a bed-pad on the sidewalk
of someone who once was homeless,
but now, you see ambitious poets like yourself
playing at being poor, pretending to be a real Indian,
or Mexican, terrified of smashing the wall down
that separates you from us, the poor and illiterate,
terrified of burning your résumé, afraid you might be taken
                                        for a commoner.

Poems are my advocates, not important enough
to appear on TV, to claim themselves the reincarnated Dali Lama
of the literary and film world,
they've humbly turned down tenure offers,
declined civic positions, rejected
distinguished commissions by government and bureaucratic bodies,
companies and organizations, associations and institutes,
gone off to walk along the lovely shore in the dawn mist
to meditate among the ebb and tide and catch sight of the dolphin.

I have no career. A poet either has a life or not,
knows in his heart the worth of poems or not,
knows if he's a fraud or not.

He said, Poems shattered my soul, words shook me.
There was no retreat, never imagine then or now
belittling my mission as a poet to that of a company poet,
someone who gets rich and famous
because a company is advertising them,

wants them to be the standard for poetry
because it doesn't upset white benefactors.

It's absurd, too common to witness
mediocre poets
picked by an organization, how the publicity department
makes the poet a pop-culture guru.
In the fame-game, you go
from anonymity to thinking yourself
literary majesty, your duty to swarm NPR and PBS stations,
weekend morning talkshows, national magazines,
advertised as the greatest
most innovative writer or poet of the century,
illustrating proof of your greatness
by counting aloud how many philanthropic grants or awards
you've stockpiled over your career.

Exotic I'm not—he went on, five kids and a mean wife,
made a living off my poetry the way
a carpenter his hammer, the welder his torch—
not haughty, not writing for Ivy-school cadets
or private-school people,
aristocratic Indian and Spanish crowds,
not a poet with clean machine-engineered credentials
or machine-manufactured poems.
Corporate wheels turn, make you acceptable, approved
by the puppet-string master,
directing you not to upset anyone, don't disagree
with grant-givers, let them manage you
by their approval measures and standards,
sign on to speaker agencies, with limo pick-ups,
literary royalty to erase your feelings of worthlessness,
your sense that your life up to that point is a disappointment.

Real poetry leads to an awareness, an open-arm vulnerability.

Today, real poets have no profession,
are derided by academics, forlorn figures
suffering from delusional self-importance,
                    but I'll tell you
what I am: a spiritual warrior on a pilgrimage
with the sincere desire to achieve council with the Gods,
air, plants, people, to dissolve
into nature and light and earth, wind and soil.

Poetry deserves total, absolute foolhardiness.

EDUCATION

゜◔） ◔゜

Overcast day, late Autumn
six of us park in the lot
tower guards and cameras monitor us
as we enter the women's prison in
McCloud, Oklahoma.

We make this trip
every month for six months
stand at the edge of the parking lot
trying to understand what prison really is
appreciate I can walk, breathe
without a guard yelling when to and how long.

Back home after a week working
with the women in writing exercises
my daughter and I juice carrots,
beets, ginger, garlic, celery, apples.
I dump rinds and fruit cores and pulp
in the compost heap
turn what's at the bottom to the sun
to take the seed in their brown hand come spring
sprout from the fertile corpse a freedom
reaching to be who they were meant to.

Going to the McCloud Women's Prison
teach reading and writing is my way of creating
acts of breaking free
in every woman who learns
to express herself.

Trust
in my speech,
linger on stories of abuse, courage, sorrow, despair—
like the young unwed mother students
at the alternative school on the first day when I walked in
these teachers have that same unknowing look
that conveys.

> I live in another world and know nothing
> about what I'm saying.
> I have no reference point, no experience,
> no lived foundation to understand them
> being mostly white.

But I slowly bring them in
to my confidence, with my poems
                    release them
from their inhibitions,
tell stories that make them realize *he knows us*,
congenial childhood narratives,
after an hour they laugh with mc,
lean forward in their chairs, eager
for more of me, hungry for more stories and poems
                    that bring us together.

An eighth grader stabbed another one
at the mid school. Parents were called
neither showed.

Following day the town
had the annual parade,
everyone showed up for the free beer.

ೞ ಄

Inside a portable classroom in Atlanta, Georgia
Mexicans and Chicanos sit at desks,
· do nothing, no books, sit there.
I tell them I'm a visiting poet,
ask what they've been doing all year,
                        they say,
                        every day, all year, sit here,
                        no teachers ever showed up.

∽⊙ ⊙∿

The rich side of town clamored for it
but she said build the library in the barrio
and they will come. She managed to get
the mayor on board, citizens, then the big boys:
                              Salinas Valley agri-giants.

The day they cut the ribbon
she told me, Oh, they will come,
you just stand there and watch,
they'll come. I was expecting a few hundred at most,
eleven thousand people—kids, mothers, fathers, grandparents
rushing in, crutches, wheelchairs, hobbling, walkers
                         to the new
                         Salinas Library
as if someone had announced they had seen La Virgen de
    Guadalupe.

I stood in awe, realized
what a central role the library has in the barrio.
From that day on I was converted,
I'd seen the holy apparition of my brown people
in love with books. Something great took hold
of my soul, the knowledge that if we bring them books,
they will come. Close quick-loan and liquor stores,
                         build more libraries
                         and we'll change the world,
                         one   book   at   a   time.

Teachers, I want you to
take away from my words
a re-commitment to re-ignite
the I-can spark in yourselves.
If it's a dim blow on your dream
to lead others into the light,
rekindle your dream from a time
when life blazed with possibilities,
blow on fire of purpose or meaning
of learning's light and share it,
step into your dream again and feed the fire,
the flame of your own potential personhood
in this world shines with brilliant illumination again.
You are the coveted fire you offer us, your students,
so we might in turn carry it and pass it on.

But it starts with you.

Carry away from my words the unwavering belief
that you are hero and messenger,
you are the seed-planting people,
going heart to heart and mind to mind,
planting the divine kernels in each student
of what they have forgotten—
who they can be in this world.

From where you sit, were you to take your finger
and trace all the way back to where you came from
as a child and remember your dream to be a teacher,
remember why you wanted to be a teacher,
then you would see yourselves again
filled with awe for life, filled with faith the world was good,
filled with the beautiful light of learning.

Education best manifests itself
in a student's ability to build a healthy
community-serving life. Education should be
the footstool that allows each student to stand above the rest,
affirm his or her best traits. A good education
creates the environment to transform what is unjust,
address when called upon to help those searching and lost.
It allows the student to wage his or her talents
compassionate heart against destructive forces
in our society, an education a student makes his or her own,
then shapes it to demolish obstacles
all of us face in making a more generous society.

It is you, teachers, all of you in this room,
who right now this very moment
carry the keys to make this marvelous
revolution possible, this transcendent crop
of young minds and hearts rising from the fields
like heady sunflowers reaching for the sun.
It is you who teach to bend but never break,
you who foster faith in themselves,
you who teach them to stay strong and determined,
and they will arrive because you are a living
and breathing testimony, a witness to that, for you're here today.

We are people who have stories to tell,
stories that need to be fulfilled,
people who have stories to share.
And in that pursuit, my amazing teachers,
your lives have been a narrative of service to others,
not for fame or fortune, but leaders on a journey
where our hearts might be fulfilled
and your commitment to your students is to fulfill
their creative potential, to help them realize
their vision in its healthiest and mindful way
of themselves serving their communities.

Ultimately, you are the keepers of the keys,
of secrets you share with students,
students who are wide-eyed and innocent,
some shy and fearful, others unable to sit
for more than minutes and always bouncing around
and inattentive, but still, you help them shape
themselves into courageous human beings and leaders.

Thank you for teaching me
and all the students who will come after me,
thank you for walking beside me,
for riding the rough days with me,
for captaining the ship of my life in stormy hurricanes,
for respecting this precious cargo called my heart,
the heaven-made box transporting my dreams
and me day by day, for you are the ones who gave me direction,
you are the ones who taught me to read
the stars in my heart and write down what they meant,
what I was capable of, who I was, where I was going
and what I could achieve, you star-readers, map makers, compass
    needles,
that kept me safely on the trail on my way to my life.
                             Thank you.

Born the moment I held a pencil
and wrote my first word,
born the first time I kissed María,
born the first time a jail cage closed me in,
born the first time I snorted cocaine,
born the first time I read a book,
born the first time I understood a poem.
Before that there was nothing,
before that there was no world,
before that there was no me,

except, perhaps, the orphanage
                     when a happy
                     part of me sprung free
from my bone marrow
one small cell sparked
bits of light in the vast darkness
as if the sun had laughed
or the moon cried,
                     the first time I was born me, in a cell,
first time illuminating my world
with light
on everything, everything,
before that there was only
darkness.

Imagine
if we taught all manner
of workpeople to read books,
imagine mechanics and tire changers,
plumbers to read poetry on a daily basis.
If we took that privilege from white trust-funders,
spread the blessings, like Marvin Gaye's songs,
to those who work with their hands,
dishwashers reading Thoreau, yardmen
reading Emerson,
secretaries reading the latest reforms
in education and maintenance people
reading law books.
Imagine a whole society of workers
reading poetry,
                              then what?
Language would come alive.

Give those who have never had books, books,
you change the world.

Let the plumber run the sentences
as he might the pipes of an old building
and bring heat,
the electrician tie the wires to bring light
to each positive and negative word,
the mason smooth the concrete to hold
a thousand eyes that pass over the words,
the carpenter lay the boards and fit the joints
for a window frame to see what once a wall obscured
                              and witness the visible
                              reaches of the unending universe
                              and kneel in awe
                                                of the word.

−≈ ≈−

Turn the classroom
into a place
where we learn
to weigh the cost of being a *pinche vendido*,
make the classroom
where we learn
que no tenemos que ser gabachos,
podemos periquear entre nosotros,
say the hardest truths *y tener confianza*
que con tiempo todo sale bien,
instead of this incessant
go-along for the *gringo*'s approval.

                          No jodas . . .

A SACK OF POTATOES, A BOWL OF APPLES

❧ ❦

Imagine having names
like this:
Avocado/
Organic bread/
Seedless Grapes/
Boneless Chuck Roast/

          They rapture me,
make me want their names:

Call me, if you see me walking down the street,
Hey, Avocado! What you doing?

And I reply,
Naw, same old same Organic Bread,
you wanna mix it up tonight at the new beet-club
maybe spread some style jams . . .

And he replies,
Maybe invite Seedless, you know,
that boy can mash up the grapes, baby . . .

And don't forget Boneless
Chuck Roast.
Anybody mess with us, he be
putting his weight on them. . . .

Yeah, okay, I reply,
get the crew
and let's cook it up.

Yeah, we stew it up.

⚜ ⚜

Set the mind aside like a black hat
that has been blown off my head
in too many storms, gone off bouncing
end over end at the mercy of winds
down too many streets, with me chasing after it
too many times, a bungling clown
in a silent black and white film.

Two Kenyans in the afternoon heat
jog down Carlisle Blvd.,
skinny black legs, yellow soiled and torn
running shoes, blue shimmery shorts,
teeth whiter than sacred hosts,
amid traffic and shoppers
so out of place in this land of consumers,
so in place in my heart.

＊ ＊

They say the crow in your dream,
seen on a yard wall or tree branch,
opens a space in you,
where, if you enter, they say,
you can hear a white crow, singing
fly with me.

ᥫᦉ ᦉᥫ

Wind blows
Buddhist flags strung across
my yard
red blue yellow
stenciled with faded words *hope, love, loneliness*
wind shakes the flags
until over time the cloth is just a blank cloth—
a life well lived.

❧ ❧

Never separate from your sadness.
It would be like the flower
separating from the rain.

꧁ ꧂

Mention whatever your mind
feels it must.
All options always end up on target
when the intention of the heart is true.

∽◎ ◎∾

My heart
my tendons
muscles, bones
held together
by the strongest substance
in the universe:

                    breath.

～❦ ❦～

One sack of potatoes
on the porch
can make the whole porch smell good.

One bowl of apples
on the counter
can make the whole kitchen
smell so good.

✦✦

Some live looking back
others looking forward
and others in the present
live.

෴ ෴

Sometimes you think
you're on top
of the world
and don't know
you're at the bottom
until you look up
at the shoe sole
about to step on you.

ود ود

When writing,
get at that beautiful abyss—
music on one end
words on the other
a Grand Canyon in between
then leap into the great void.

ALLOW THE ANGELS IN

The secret
is not how many possessions
you bring into your life,
how many friends or awards
or parties you attend,
how many commendations or drugs
or girlfriends or new cars
you have.

It's what you quit, leave behind,
words you used to hurt others,
the resentments,
the ambitions that bring you
false glory and vanity,
the power you seek with your nice clothes
and gym-built body.

Life can be understood
in two versions:
the boy in scruffy clothes and ill-fitting
shoes and dirty hair,
little arms and fingers
crusted with play dirt from the field
and sandbox, face round and smiling,
the big head with thick black hair,
the small legs and scruffy kneecaps . . .
little boy with a small voice and big eyes

And

the warrior prison created,
the vengeful mutha who wouldn't
hesitate to take on anyone
no matter the color or size

if he crossed my path
in an arrogant manner
he'd be mine.

When I quit him
said goodbye to that part of me,
let the boy resume his life,
see through his innocent heart,
I opened a door that allowed angels in . . .

cð ගා

Poetic Prayer

Lord,
during this period of quarantine
and social distancing,
let me swirl my poetic concoction
and brew up an elixir
that'll mount an attack on ignorance
and enlighten the disbelievers.

cða ᏩᎧ

You who cannot forgive,
do not conceal your grievance,
do not withhold your affection

because of what happened or didn't.

Raise yourself
to the occasion of your full self,
engage your forgiveness
                                        forged
in your willingness to experience
sadness and joy. . . .
Life is brief, my dear, in the snap of a finger, it's gone.

Rise.

Eleven years in an orphanage.

Playground nuns rang the bell
swung it up and down with effort
signaled the end of play day
kids streamed in in ragged clusters
from all points on the playground—sandboxes,
monkey bars, slides, whirly helicopter
with long dangling chains one kid lapped
over the others and we all ran in unison
                              around and around
until we all snapped our chains
sending the kid skyward
sailing and flung toward the angels,
as he held on tight to his handle
gripped his iron bar at the end of the chain
looked down at all our awed faces
looking up at him high in the sky
then we dashed, grouped by ages
under the corrugated shed
marched in line on the sidewalk
to the washroom with the massive concrete tubs
where we scrubbed the dirt off our faces and hands
then waited in the adjoining playroom
for our group sister to lead us to the dining room.

The abandoned playground, dining room,
hallways, waited for us to come out
and play and eat and rough-house
down the halls and stairs—everything
conjured a caldron-stirring
waiting for us if only for a moment in a day.

On Sunday I waited by the gate
for mother to arrive, waited for years
standing there holding the wrought iron
in my tiny hands, searching each car and truck
as they arrived thinking the next would be my mother
be my mother be my mother I yearned
and it never was: eleven years, the bars,
the gate, the lock, me looking out through them,
standing on the inside watching and looking out
at the world of people come and go,
only the playground and dining room and hallways
healing me, all the way through prison, where years later
I stood at the bar looking out, waiting, still waiting.

At four
I sat on yard dirt
played with stick patches
with fire I called mother
with smoke I called father

I intoned my chants and whispers
on the air and wind and sun
implored the lonely September morning
its hawks to give hawk-blessings
horny-toad talk
tumbleweed rolls
ant stings and grasshopper flings

then grandma called me in
for nap time
I drowsed to the howling prairie silence
creeping through the newspapered cracks
in the walls
of our tar-paper two-room shack

waking I'd go out
lay back on the ground again
growling stick and stone wars
toward dusk, breeze
shivers me
the Manzano mountains to the east
blow down the smell of snow
I know
                    I come from up there.
                    Part of me
                    is made of
                    that mountain.

＊

Definitions of Happiness:

A word used to sell an unfulfilled person
spiritual sweeteners, guaranteeing
a quick-fix, painless existence.

To exploit the unsuspecting.

A wanton, snot-nosed runt
abused by a sudden flush of elation,
an uprising state of mind
that gives a momentary reason to live.

Think
how some live by information
from the world.
Read it, catalogue, store it,
build on it, attach our lives to it,
depend on it.

Lose spontaneity.

Others live by the information
from their feelings,
leap up and down, never grounded,
retain the child in themselves.

Some by ideas so angry (racism),
they go blind
even though they see.

Those who gather information
from all three
then release it like brown and white doves
to the sky, watch from their balcony
returning again their innocence,

even wonder.

ɹ◌ ◌ɹ

Us
damaged goods when we met
somehow
salvaged
remnants of hope, work with less
live with less—no inheritance
no relatives to help with kids
day to day digging in
never enough for bills or food
learned to love a strong way, our hearts
brimming bowls we served the other
savoring every morsel
every touch and kiss, at the end of each day
                              licking our fingers.

ॐ ॐ

If you listen intently
your heart will answer the call, like
sunrise coming over the cliffs.
Watch the sun hit a distant peak in your heart,
slowly it comes into sight.
Watch it slowly illuminate this incredibly lovely land
                                    called your life.

⁊⁊ ⁊⁊

Everything's getting closed in,
there's a sense you better do something
to get yourself together.
If you don't, all hell's gonna break loose.
That's where the story comes in, your story,
it's the only thing that can calm the tiger,
only thing to dampen the flames,
only thing to stop the walls and ceiling
from burning you alive is the story.

People need to tell a story, for whatever reason.
Something in them drives them—
incessant whispers, hisses, snarls, claws—
to tell and there's more telling
in the frayed, torn, patched overcoat
of a marijuana smuggler than in most
ambitious, award-winning
nose-ring huff & puff careerists
luxuriating in academic arrangements.

WILDLIFE

In Attenborough's "Our Planet"
documentary, when I saw the baby penguin
waiting for his mother to return with food,
waiting in the arctic blizzard, staring into the whiteout
for months, not moving, not wavering, not an inch,
waiting for mother, I realized we all have our roles
in our relationship to mother earth.

                                         Break from our
roles and we disturb if not shatter the sacred ring
that binds us all, that ensures our continuance,
that gives us our soul, our integrity, our reason for being.

When Attenborough filmed the walruses
hundreds of thousands trying to fit onto one small island,
many crushed, many died, those who somehow bellied up
to the cliffs for room to rest, high up above the sea,
when it was time to leave, they gazed down at the water
and each one sailed off the cliffs to their deaths,
driven by ancient migration patterns, propelled by instinct
deep in their cells, it was horrible to watch them
wriggling mid-air then slamming into the reefs below,
dying a terrible, excruciating death
because humans have taken their habitat,
destroyed their homes.

And those beautiful orangutans,
driven like felons and fugitives to one small island,
their numbers, like the walruses and penguins, cut in half
and their lands ruined by our commercial greed for more
and more and more and more,
makes me want to strike out and destroy cities,
destroy buildings, destroy countries, makes me want
to give it back to them,
the trees, the ants, the fish, the polar bears ask only

for ice, the orangutans have a few miles of tropical forest left
developed for palm oil.
                                    Whatever we touch we murder.
And it's not good enough to care anymore,
it's not enough to converse with friends
about climate change, it's not enough to write about it,
we must rise to the occasion, object to the murdering
of wolves, of whales, of air, wind, fire and water.
We must.

cഗ Gഄ

Morning prayer, after running
three miles yesterday in the foothills,
lovely are the toes that squinched
to balance me
on a million occasions,
lovely the ankles that strained
up hills, forest paths, on rocks,
lovely the calves that muscled thick
from running a thousand miles
and knees that bent, kept their rocker arms
moving for me as I gasped and exhaled in
miles and miles of Río Grande river air,
lovely are the thighs that gripped and released,
clenched and opened over rock and trail and bend and rise,
taking me to the summit where I stood and thanked
the four elements for their blessings.

꧁ ꧂

I never learned anything in the right place. I could not sit
in astronomy class in school. I had to go outside
under the night sky and stare until my eyes blurred.
I always found myself in the wrong place learning by experience
what others learned in the right places through books or parents.
Rocks? I went hiking for days. Filled my pockets.
Water? I went searching for springs. Quenched my thirst. Drank
    at the source.

Wednesdays when the trash truck arrives
dogs in the barrio go crazy barking at them
and I think
if only humans did as much
when people pollute.

cn◎ ⊙ఎ

On my hike
ponderosas and junipers
welcome my footsteps
on Autumn's twig and leaf trail,
black rosary beads of morning dew dangle
from the shivering fingers of nun-cedars.

Autumn leaves turn red
proof red was there all the time,
as the days progress the tiger's eye opens wider
in the leaves. . . .

                        Meditate
                        the wind whispers
                        use your breath,
                        the fire flashes
                                    inhale, exhale
                        the water says
                        blow, the earth says
                        let the tiger out.

Buffalo Prayer

Prairie flowers bloom
in hoof ruts
in depressed traces in the grass
visible where we

                          once roamed.

Feels good to go forward,
feels good to give to the two-legged,
to trample what separates us, stampede
religious beliefs with the beauty of ourselves—

                          we left trails
                          for you to follow–

hoof scratch, grip-gash, pinch-push
our ancient hieroglyphic scripture in the dirt,
inscribe on mother's body
our ministry of love and surrender. . . .

                          We left trails
                          for you to follow.

Buffalo Dance

Heat the prairie
hooves engrave it
agitate air, sky, earth
   with a coming
with heat made hooves
heat-hooves sure as flames
sure as hot red coals
sure as orange/yellow and red
   buffalo
heart blows the energy of fire
mixed with stars and sun
   blows
huffs warmth on the world
ribs skull horns hooves
embrace the air, the earth, the light
strenuous tendon fibers
bones and muscle crackle
cracking whatever lays between
   to remind us one
black snouts and teeth trailed
with bits of wild carrots/blueberries/prairie grass
vegetal peelings
hooves so hot
chisel air with crystal waves
that blur us
to water and fire alive
   in the ceremony of living
as dancer to flute
so hoof to earth
   breathe   breathe   breathe
rolling into the storm
   they come
   awakening us in the grace of their being
   in the music of their drum beating hooves

shaping us into our humanity
carving us back to our prairie-self
with the message
respect, be conscious, listen

we are brothers, sisters
more heat, more hoof, more breath
   more heart
hoof music heats us back
to our essence, to our nature of light
to our nature of wind and rain
   to the fire
from where we come
   to the spirit
   we share
   with them.

Buffalo Poem

All over the city
I hear the
explosive sounds
rat-ta-ra-boom—and—nostrils blowing
chesthuffsheaving

                         Buffalo are coming
shuddering air, dust trails
smoke across sky
spreading dirt clouding the air
streams over housetops
obscures skyscrapers and stars
TVs flicker then fuzz
disrupt Netflix movies making mindless fools
grab guns and shoot away, grab knives and slice
clubs and bludgeon and bombing. . . .

                         Buffalo are coming
furry, bulky bodies avalanche
hooves thunder rumbling pavement
crack streets, toppling streetlights
hemorrhaging traffic, exits jammed
marshal law declared
armored military goon-squads in Bradley tanks
roam the night
with orders to kill the four-hoofed creature, but

                         Buffalo are coming
down the Appalachia trail and Continental Divide
grinding false patriots beneath typhoon hooves
stampeding metal weapons, money, power. . . .

                                        Buffalo are coming
across the Grand Canyon, splashing
over Niagara Falls
spanning one end of the world to the other

                                        Buffalo are coming
smashing homes and hearts
waking people, stirring them to think
to feel again, to do away with profit margins. . . .

                                        Buffalo are coming
in New Mexico, where I am, I see them
friends call they see them too—
New Hampshire woods, Seattle shoreline,
Indiana's mountaintops, Minnesota lakes—

                                        Buffalo are coming
cross deserts and Kansas corn fields
cross Alabama football fields
Florida golf courses, Southern California beaches
flattening New York City gyms, crushing
treadmills, stationary bicycles and elliptical machines.

And as the sun rises over the cliffs and on my cabin
here I am, lying on my side.
I watch the sun hit a distant peak
slowly it comes into sight— emerges from dusk
then it's time to get up
and get the day's chores done.

But this morning

                                        a White Buffalo
stands visible in the Autumn mist, and I dash out.
It approaches me in my pasture, and I give it a slap
on the rump and it bolts off

through forest trees
and watching it, I have a desire to follow
answer it—
its voice spoke to me the way fire talks with darkness:

        Get on with lighting you up, it said,
gristle and knees, shoulders and neck
stomach and fingers, its voice spread throughout me
one beautiful smooth spreading of light
                live as a human
                live as human
                live as human.

When I sit on the porch
and listen to the running creek
it sounds like a dog licking it paws
sore from running all day in the fields.

My Prayer to the Buffalo

Gentle heart you are
           I would say
sumo-sweetness, the prairie breeze
so bracing it recalls your soul
to times you ambled in amber citrus fields down south
              where fragrant fields
nose black as a grape
dangle upward on a vine of wind
enjoying the scent of red, orange and yellow
             your heart
             tenderly folding around the afternoon
             like fresh corn leaves
             wrapping a tamal.

Gentle heart you are
             four Directions open to you
             your prickly scruff fur
             rough as pineapple skin
             the yellow in your eye
             mango soft
             you offer yourself
             to the Four Directions
to all
             who are hungry
even those who had forgotten the sacred language of Respect
who had forgotten the sacred ceremony of Living
who came and slaughtered and upset the balance
             unprotected.
Gentle heart that you are
first cutting, second cutting, third cutting
each successive generation got thinner and thinner
until you almost became extinct
             but the People remembered
             how children called you Big Leaf

how adults remembered you were called Full Beauty
how the medicine men and healer women
took Four Drops of Blood from you
and mixed them with dirt from Four Directions
and then they prayed
they prayed, prayed prayed prayed prayed
standing all night on a mountain, in a prairie, at a forest, by the shore
they prayed they prayed they prayed they prayed

until Your Gentle Heart unfolded
its leaves again, giving off a peppery mintiness on the breeze
and the People danced
practiced Your old ways
sang Your songs
made You gifts
cared again for the land
told stories around the fire again, grandfather to father to child
and again you multiplied
pizza and soda pops and cornbread were brought
to the pow-wows, eggs, almonds, pinons
even English muffins and white bread
and La Gente ate and danced and sang in thanks
that Gentle Hearts roamed among them again.

Buffalo Rain

Strong rain. Big, hard masculine drops
smack the canyon forest pines. I hear
a black-nostril'd heave sigh over the fields.

In the meadow beyond my cabin
buffalo rain grazes in the morning mist,
nibbles withered grass tips,
wrenches at the day-moon
hanging in dew on twigs.

The buffaloes clomp
over the once-new 2x4's
I was going to use building the dog pen,
blackened by a year's weather in the weeds.

A Hopi friend tells me
gnarly white ginger roots
I'm planting this year
are buffalo-spirit hooves
that dig at earth until it thaws through
to release
barrel-chested healthy nubs.

I think of this as I watch
buffalo rain
in the same meadows
kids from the village
brought O'Keefe to,
where she found the colors she dreamed of
for her painting.

The children told her what each flower was,
its medicinal and ceremonial use,
how the petals sweep
the blue from the sky and save the sky in its roots/petals.
(Imagine saving sky . . . the way you do pennies in a jar!)
They taught her Chicano/Indio names,
instructed her in the ways of grandmothers
distilling pigments from blossoms and stems.
Without them, there'd be no O'Keefe paintings
as we know them.

⋞⋟ ⋞⋟

In the 1850s the village was a trading post
where Hopis, Utes, Apaches, Comancheros
Kiowa, Dene, a few Crow and Lakota
traded captives and horses,
a village (not a pueblo). Mexicans
and Indios married, and today we have more tribes
living side by side than anywhere else.

They say O'Keefe painted the cliffs
behind my cabin and sold the canyon series
for millions to Kemper Museum in Kansas City.
Made her famous and wealthy,
while the villagers were given oranges
and thought they were eating tiny suns.

The same cliffs
I pray to each morning, same cliffs where my ancestors
appear each night in ghost form, dancing and praying.
I see them when I go hiking,
two hundred-year-old young couples sitting in boulders
scooped out by centuries of rain, kissing.
Meet my uncle spirit hunters in other boulders
carved out with stone chisels,
sit in and wait for elk or turkey to come by.
In some boulders chiseled by wind,
young warriors perch as lookouts
for raiding parties.
Some ground rocks have been whittled smooth
to divert rainwater to gather in designated pools.

I visit these sacred places and pray,
nod to my ancestors—*tíos, tías, abuelo/as y padres*—
see them as clearly as I do my hand.

I thank them for permitting me to be here.

Each morning I ask them for guidance.
Each morning I offer my heart to them.

Later, I catch the morning news,
where viral hornets are swarming cities.
                    Nature, I think,
self-correcting what we haven't,
balancing people out of whack,
arrives to clean house.

Gives Mother Earth a reprieve from our greed.
Pollution decreases. Traffic lessens. Power Mongers
pause grunting at the trough—
no more maddening gotta-have this gotta-do that,
no more gluttonous consumption of oil,
no more guzzling consumers,
—not a nuclear bomb or white dictator
that's come to destroy,
but a tiny invisible microscopic

                              leveler,
                              balancer.
We expected Brown People, Chicanos and Mexicans,
we caged them, separated families, murdered them.
We imagined them wielding weapons: drugs, alcohol, bombs.
They warned us these would be the enemy
but an aerial corona star appears in the blood
to settle the books,
empty every commercial establishment,
force humans to cower behind locked doors.

The enemy didn't come at us crossing borders,
swinging machetes and machine guns.
A benign emperor embracing us in groups and crowds,
merging into our breathing, in his glittering carriage, came.

Far from the closest person,
I've only spoken a few words in thirty years,
in this womb of cliffs.
Silence is the language I speak,
suspends its mist over everything.

I stand on the porch
listening to the raindrops
tick the green galvanized roof.

Some leaves
didn't fall this winter,
clutter the boughs
still trying to clutch onto spring,
to what they had,
to what they were, and their failure's
meaning of life
is to surrender—
nothing holds on to what it had,
to what it was.

Gust-clusters strong enough to shove me back
hackle the crackly beige leaves,
make Bella (my Corso) turn
searching animal movement,
catching a whiff. She lunges tongue-long
growling after ancestral spirits that kindle the air,
tracking their glittering with sniffs
over boulders into the weeds,
dashing up a wildlife trail,
baptized by brush,
sparkling rain on her.

I watch
and the silence whispers:
Do not hold on to what you had,
to who you were.

Live light.

The Time of Gardens

When the Corona virus hit
Leo, the toothless hound
could no longer pick up aging white women
at the gym and shortly after had a nervous breakdown.

Hustlers on street corners sold toilet paper
instead of drugs
and the rate of addiction went way down.

Neighbors wearing Make America Great Again hats
ordered truckloads of rocks
and built fences and walls to keep the virus out.

The birthrate went way down.

Rich liberal whites installed titanium seatbelts
in their Teslas to strap in their tea-cup poodles.

And even, it was heard, that the mother viruses
had micro-seatbelts installed in their colonies
telling with delight their children viruses
that it was going to get real crazy
since most Americans were unprepared for the shit
that was going to hit the fan, so, strap in, sweeties!

Also, viral baby-strollers sold out,
as viral births were in the gazillions
and viruses celebrated
in their human hosts—think of Brazil's Carnival,
and multiply that by a trillion trillion trillion viruses
feasting and dancing on the human immune system!

∞ ∞

Schools closed
for the first time in memory.
Kids were happy as freed prisoners.

People showing up in emergency rooms
with no bed-capacity
watched Netflix on their mobile phones,
slept on each other like in a cell.

The homeless lined the sidewalks
wrapped in toilet paper to keep warm.
Didn't stink, they had nice, clean warm butts.

No one took the holy wafer at Sunday Mass
and no one went to hell.

Grass grew green, flowers bloomed,
dogs sunned comfortably on patios,
and since gatherings were banned
and travel discouraged, people could be seen
reading books again.

Public health services were dismally lacking
or non-existent (our leader in-chief had gone into hiding)
and people learned to take care
of themselves, eating right, exercising outside, walking
and hiking and smiling again.

And what's crazy about all of this? When the wealthy
got on their jets and yachts and hid on their private islands,
gangster viruses hunted them down and took them out—

I mean, how cool is that, right?

It was almost like, in the midst of the pandemic crises
people remembered they were human, they had time to think
again, they had time to spend with kids,
they had time to evaluate their lives and the choices
they made, and change came about. They realized
the jobs they had were wasting their time
and the money they spent on tuition and malls and prescriptions
was not needed.

And slowly, the people came out into the sun
and laughed, as if some great enlightenment
had befallen the population, and citizens everywhere,
even prisoners in prison, started writing letters again
to those they hadn't spoken to in years.
People tried to find each other to ask for forgiveness.
Shovels came out of garden sheds
and soon gardens were spreading where before
there were only dirt lots.

And believe it not, buffalos appeared
in parks to graze.

It was a time future generations would later call
the time of gardens.

Yesterday, clambering, ducking,
crawling on all fours, bending,
getting snagged on branches, scratched,
briars tangling my boots, closing my eyes
to pass through a nest of wild thorny vines
and stickered stems,
I came upon a depressed oval grass mat
where a bear slept,
scat circling the rim, big black seeded
lumps of bear poop—I touched it, soft
to my fingertips, made me feel blessed.

When I got back to my cabin, I took off my shirt
to get ready to shower
and aspen leaves
showered down from my shoulders
onto the floor.
           The mountain
           gave me a parting gift.

ೞ ൭

I hiked eleven miles yesterday
up steep mountainous terrain
(with my Mexican friend Vidal)
searching for springs to tap
to feed fresh mountain water down to
the fields.
     Shouldered up trails,
crouched up through,
clambered over massive sycamore logs
fallen with their huge army of branches. Trunks
heavier and larger than semi-trucks wrenched
out of earth dwarfed me, standing next to their
upended roots.

I wonder how bears
can do this, giant and brawny as they are,
how do they keep moving through miles and miles
of underbrush so thick and impenetrable,
being so massive?

Fighting your way slowly for hours
through scrawl-briars, razored bushes,
the nicks, the gouges, the piercings, the hot
sting of thorns, bleeding where the claws
puncture your skin, unaware of where
you are, how to get back, how to get out, how to
find your way, your fear becomes another wound,
and for an instant worry
flushes you with the fever of being lost
never finding your way again.

But six hours and eleven miles later,
boot-sucking in streams and kneeling under
branches, eyes alert so I don't gash an eye

or rip my face on a sharp stick or dead talons of wood, forward
into the wilderness of impassable burrs,
so dense I can't see beyond arm's reach, knees
tired, ankles aching, lungs exhausted,
gasping hard, resting to inhale and expel
huge gulps of air, I carry on,
crawling on knees and hands uphill,
mounds of bear skat everywhere, mauled bird remains,
mats of feathers scattered about on the ground
in the twigs and leaves,
finally I find the wildlife trail leading

> back down the mountain.

At the cabin—no matter how slow I move,
fingers blistered, hands, thighs, back scratched,
drying scabs on forearms, hamstrings seized with cramps,
joints hurting—I don't bother to apply
antibiotic ointment to all the tiny stabs and cuts
that razor-nick my neck and cheeks.
I consider them the down of tiny feathers
stuck to bird shell fragments, speckled
with afterbirth slime and blood,
after the bird hatched within its egg,

> and taken

> an exhilarating first flight

and now landed, making my way to the shower,
don't know if I'll ever
be content to just walk again.

There is no judgement or competition.
We all fly in our own way.

After the rigorous hike
white sweat stains drying on my baseball cap and t-shirt—
the best work, sucks out from the flesh
body juices better
than any sport, makes you feel
you've won, you've participated in living
and filled the day an honorable way.

I wake up in the night, take a deep, gruff
belly and chest breath, my breath
comes out solid, heavy and strong, a conscious presence
swollen with tree, boulder, water and earth
of its own being,
fills the room with its wildlife personality,
breath I do not recognize as my own, breath
more like the bear's in winter sleep,
after huffing and grubbing fallen logs, turning over boulders,
eating a canyon-brimming amount of wild berries, wipes its
paws
clawing inch deep cuts up tree trunks—
a husky, powerful movement
of air that engages my whole body, issues from deep
within me, expelling something that doesn't belong there,
emptying me of something not needed,
something now gone,
that has emptied me, makes room
for the mountain to settle in, curl down and hibernate
inside my back, shoulder and thighs,
                                            next to my heart.

When I am hiking
the throat is the place
where words become birds.

cr⊙ ⊙ﾟ

Driving in last night, my son
saw a young bear by the gate. It trundled off
as if caught stealing something, its large
boom-boom butt
lunging hind-right to hind-left
in escape down the dirt road, up the hills
into cedar and pines. I tell my son (17)
it's a blessing.

This morning,
a touch of holiness on the forehead
and heart—finches dart in and out of impassable
bramble brush without a single feather
nicking one thorned twig.

One morning (true story)
early spring
I walk out to the compost pit,
step barefooted within an inch or two
of a dozen rattlers with tails hissing,
my naked heel within an inch of them.

                                    Not one bit me.
The earth knows me
in a way it knows her creatures
in her world.
Ending has no name, not death or gone or lived once.
The bear, finch and rattlesnake
come without a name for living and dying.
The absence of it
is the meaning of a life lived.

⌘ ⌘

Running the foothills
the wind rises,
trees sway and I think
nothing can stop, hold, overwhelm
or challenge the wind,
except one power which is fiercer,
more commanding:

Silence.

                    It contains the wind.

Hiking
I study the hills
where plants and boulders
cling to steep inclined earth, have to tilt
over at awkward angles to remain,
from falling over, to survive,
to keep from losing their hold
grip niches in rock cracks
to keep from blowing away,
sage, cacti, grass, creosote, mesquite, cedar
tunnel root-tendons like soft bones
deep in sandy granite hillside,
no matter the winds, rains, drought, heat,
they keep staying—living sideways, holding on,
                    a weathered example
                    of being grateful for what one has,
gives me courage to keep clinging to hope and to learn
                    life's most important lesson:
practice how to lean in life so as not to fall,
to root and exist on the incline of life
embrace adversity with constant tenacity.

Also by Jimmy Santiago Baca

A Glass of Water

A Place to Stand

American Orphan

Black Mesa Poems

Breaking Bread with the Darkness:
Book 1: The Esai Poems

Feeding the Roots of Self Expression

The Heat: Steelworker Lives & Legends

The Importance of a Piece of Paper: Stories

Immigrants in Our Own Land &
Selected Early Poems

Laughing in the Light

Martín and Meditations on the South Valley: Poems

Rita and Julia

Selected Poems / Poemas Selectos

Singing at the Gates: Selected Poems

Spring Poems Along the Rio Grande

Stories from the Edge

When I Walk Through That Door, I Am: An Immigrant
Mother's Quest for Freedom